This book belongs to

....

MURILLA GORILLA
AND THE
HAMMOCK PROBLEM

JENNIFER LLOYD
ILLUSTRATED BY JACQUI LEE

SIMPLY READ BOOKS

To Pierre, Patrick and Emily. For encouraging and laughing along with Murilla. —J. Lloyd

For Mom and Dad, my two biggest fans. —J. Lee

Published in 2014 by Simply Read Books
www.simplyreadbooks.com

Text © 2014 Jennifer Lloyd

Illustrations © 2014 Jacqui Lee

Library and Archives Canada Cataloguing in Publication
Lloyd, Jennifer, author
Murilla Gorilla and the hammock problem /
written by Jennifer Lloyd ; illustrated by Jacqui Lee.

ISBN 978-1-927018-47-7 (bound)

I. Lee, Jacqui, illustrator II. Title.

PS8623.L69M873 2014   jC813'.6   C2013-906056-1

We gratefully acknowledge for their financial support of our publishing program the Canada Council for the Arts, the BC Arts Council, and the Government of Canada through the Canada Book Fund (CBF).

Manufactured in Malaysia

Book design by Naomi MacDougall

10 9 8 7 6 5 4 3 2 1

Contents

Chapter 1
Breakfast 5

Chapter 2
The Hammock Problem 11

Chapter 3
Something Fishy 17

Chapter 4
Strange Tracks 25

Chapter 5
Time for a Disguise! 29

Chapter 6
Still Hungry 39

Chapter 1
Breakfast

The sun was up over the African Rainforest.

Murilla Gorilla was hungry.

She opened her fridge. The top shelf was empty. The bottom shelves were empty. Something was on the middle shelf.

It was an old shoe!

"I can't eat this! Time to go shopping! I must go to Mango Market."

Murilla Gorilla is a detective. She never knows when she will have to solve a mystery.

Just in case, she brought her detective backpack.

GRR! Murilla's tummy rumbled as she drove to Mango Market. Murilla went straight to Ms. Chimpanzee's muffin stall.

"*MMM.* Those muffins look good," said Murilla to Ms. Chimpanzee.

"Murilla! You do not have time to eat muffins! Okapi is upset. He has a case for you. You should go to his hammock stall right away."

GRR! Murilla's tummy rumbled
some more.

"What was that noise?"
asked Ms. Chimpanzee.

"I did not eat breakfast," said Murilla.

"Have a muffin to go," offered
Ms. Chimpanzee.

Murilla took a bite of the muffin.

"Murilla! Hurry!"

"I am on my way," Murilla said.

Chapter 2
The Hammock Problem

Murilla never rushed.

"Hello," she said to Tree Frog, sitting on a branch.

"Good morning," she said to Mandrill.

"Nice new parasols!" she yelled out to Parrot at his stall.

Crocodile and Croc Junior were walking down the path towards the river. Crocodile waved to Murilla but Croc Junior did not.

Croc Junior must be feeling shy this morning, thought Murilla.

At last, Murilla arrived at
Okapi's Hammocks.

"What's wrong?"
Murilla asked Okapi.

He pointed to a hammock.
It had a hole in the middle.

"Why are you selling a hammock
with a hole in it?" asked Murilla.

"Murilla, I am not selling a hammock with a hole in it! I left my stall to go shopping. When I came back, I found a hole in this hammock! By the way, do you need a hammock with a hole in it? This one is half price."

"No, thank you. How do you think it happened?"

"Murilla! That's what I want YOU to find out!"

In her notebook, Murilla drew a picture of a hammock with a hole in it.

Chapter 3
Something Fishy

"Time to look for clues.
I need my magnifying glass."

Murilla looked in her backpack.
She pulled out something
round with a long handle.

She held it up to the hammock.
But she did not see the hammock.
Instead, she saw herself.

"Why are you looking in a mirror?"
asked Okapi.

"Oops!"

Murilla put back the mirror and took
out her magnifying glass.

She leaned in close to the hammock.

She looked through the hole.

Murilla saw something black.

It was hairy. It had five toes.

Murilla jumped! The black thing jumped!

"Do you see a clue?" asked Okapi. He leaned in close to have a look.

"Murilla, that is your foot!"

"Oops!"

Murilla was embarrassed. She kept checking the hammock.

SNIFF! SNIFF!
"What is that smell?"

SNIFF! SNIFF!
"I know that smell."

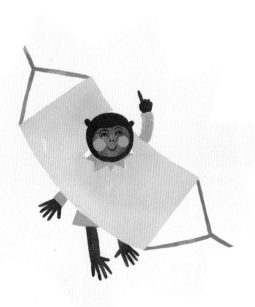

At last Murilla figured it out.
The hammock smells like fish!

"Okapi, did you put a fish on
your hammock?"

"No! Why would I do that?
I only eat leaves."

That gave Murilla an idea.

*Maybe an animal that eats a lot
of fish slept on Okapi's hammock.*
In her notebook, Murilla drew a fish.

Chapter 4
Strange Tracks

Murilla walked away from *Okapi's Hammocks.*

"Where are you going?" asked Okapi.

"To the river," said Murilla.

"Why?"

"That's where there are fish."

Okapi looked confused. He followed her anyway.

BUMP!

"Murilla, why did you stop?"

"Because I see a clue. Look.
There are footprints in the mud."

Murilla counted them,
"One, two, three, four."

The first two were big.
The second two were small.

In her notebook, Murilla tried
to draw an animal with two big
front feet and two small back feet.

It was hard.

Chapter 5
Time for a Disguise!

At the edge of the river,
Murilla opened her backpack.

She pulled out her water lily disguise.

"Not right!"

She pulled out her mermaid disguise.

"Not right, either!"

At last, she pulled out the one she
needed.

She put it on and waded into the water.

"Murilla, why are you dressed as a giant fish?" asked Okapi.

"*SHH!* I am trying to catch an animal with two big feet and two small feet that eats fish."

Okapi sighed. Murilla waited.

THUMP! THUMP! Murilla heard
loud footsteps!

It was Elephant coming to drink.

"His feet are all the same size!
Not him!"

THUMP! THUMP!
More footsteps.

It was Hippo filling her bucket.

"Her feet are all the same size, too! Not her!"

Just then, Murilla heard another sound.

Crocodile and Croc Junior swam past Murilla.

SNIFF! *SNIFF!* "There is that smell again!"

Murilla watched them climb out onto the shore, first Crocodile and then Croc Junior.

She could see their footprints!

"Two big front prints and two small back prints!"

Okapi saw the tracks too.

"Crocodile and Croc Junior, wait!"
called Murilla.

Crocodile turned around.

"Murilla, why are you dressed
like a fish?"

"Never mind! Did you put a hole
in Okapi's hammock?"

"No, but I did let Croc Junior
have a nap in the hammock
while I did my shopping."

Murilla looked at Croc Junior.

"Did you put a hole in Okapi's hammock?"

Croc Junior hid behind Crocodile.

"Croc Junior?" said Crocodile.

"Yes, I made the hole. I did not mean to. I think that I took a bite out of the hammock while I was dreaming about eating fish. I am sorry, Okapi."

Chapter 6
Still Hungry

Later, Murilla went to check on Okapi.

"Okapi, where did your ripped hammock go?"

"Crocodile and Croc Junior sewed up the hole. Then Crocodile bought it from me. He wanted Croc Junior to have a comfy place to nap."

Talking about naps made Murilla tired. "Time to head home!"

She walked towards her car.

GRR! Murilla's tummy rumbled again.

"Oops!" She almost forgot.

She had some shopping to do first.